A CROW'S TALE

WRITTEN AND ILLUSTRATED BY SUSIE SMART

Susie Smart

ISBN: 1451518889
ISBN 13: 9781451518887
LCCN: 2010903008

To Isaiah and Griffin
Two very Best Friends

And Thanks to Hon and Sid for
Teaching me to Love Nature

Folks call us common, but what do they know?
The thoughts that go on in the mind of a crow.

My best friend Isaiah and I, Griffin's my name,
decided one day our lives were quite lame.

We live by a beach in the Pacific Northwest,
up in a fir tree in a large twiggy nest.

The water was wonderful, the rocks and the sand,

but the gulls that all live there we simply can't stand!

They're loud and they're pushy, messy and rude.
They take over the beach and eat all the food.

They are the thing that inspired our game.
Because of the gulls, our lives would not be the same.

Being crows we just love to have fun,
like flying on warm winds up towards the sun.

Fly away from the coast, leave the ocean behind,
go on an adventure to see what we'd find.

We flew to the east, flew for days it did seem,

had to go down and get drinks from a stream.

We'd crossed the tall Coast Range, when Isaiah let out a caw!
You would not believe the sight that we saw!

A beautiful valley all patch-worked in green.
More houses and people than I'd ever seen.

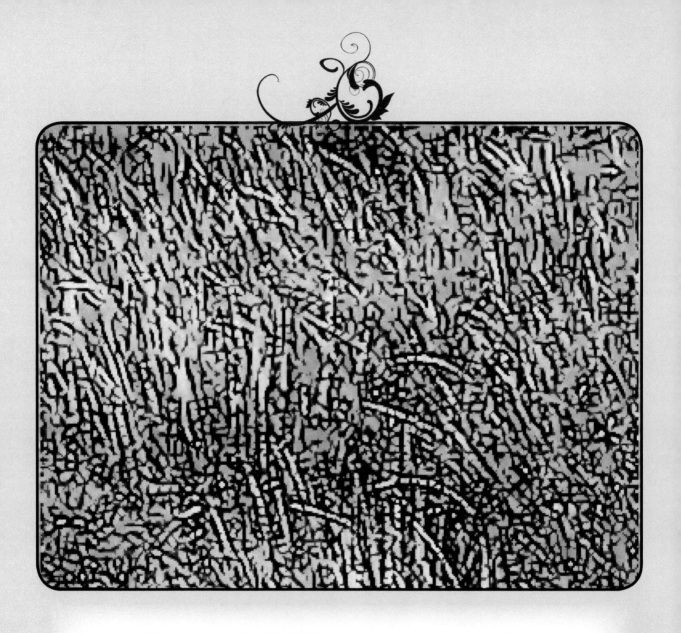

There were fields full of corn, grasses and wheat,

we thought it was time to get something to eat.

We sat on a butte with a view to the west,

just sat there awhile to give us a rest.

A murder of crows came up from below.
That's what they call us, but why? I don't know.

The group was real friendly, and one was real sweet.
Maybe she'd know where we'd get something to eat.

"I know a place where you could be led,
where the people have peanuts," is what she then said.

"There's water, cracked corn and sunflower seed,
I'll take you there now, it's just what you need."

We flew to a house, in the yard we would land.

A lady came out with peanuts in hand.

Our new friend, her name it was Kit,
showed us around and just where to sit.

We knew we were safe to go there each day,
to see the peanut lady. "Hello," she would say.

We fed there all Summer and into the Fall.
We'd go with the murder when we heard them call,

We three stayed together through Winter till Spring,
when all of the birds started to sing.

We made lots of friends, it wasn't that hard,
for life was abundant way down in that yard.

There are Fox squirrels and Scrub jays, a Stellar jay too.
Sparrows and Mourning doves with their wonderful coo.

Bushtits and Hummers, a Blackcap named Dee.
We hear him call out from up in the tree.

We sit in the evening and watch the sun set,
And remember the day when we had first met.

The weather is warmer, and life is the best,
I think it is time to help kit build a nest.

Isaiah has found himself a new friend,
But I'll always be his best one,
From beginning to END.

There's a place in the deep woods,

just under the butte,

With injured Eagles and Horned owls,

we hear them go hoot!

"The people have saved them," I heard someone say,

Built them a great home, a safe place to stay.

I met a smart crow there, his name might be Poe
He taught me of language, I now say Hello!

CASCADES RAPTOR CENTER is a 501c3 non-profit Nature Center and Wildlife Hospital for birds of prey in Eugene Oregon. Through wildlife rehabilitation and public education, CRC fosters a connection between people and birds of prey. Their goal is to help the human part of the natural community learn to value, understand and honor the role of wildlife in preserving the natural and cultural heritage of the Pacific Northwest. They have worked with over 2500 birds in the last 17 years, returning nearly 1300 to the wild.

Part of the profits in the sale of this book go to support the CASCADES RAPTOR CENTER.

I live in Eugene Oregon, just below the South hills and Spencer Butte.

My husband and I call our back yard the home entertainment center. We have bird and squirrel feeders and lots of bird baths.

About six years ago a pair of crows started coming into the yard to feed on the peanuts we give to the squirrels. Shy at first, then becoming accustomed to me and my voice they came every day and I would toss them the peanuts. I always call hello to them.

The next Spring they brought their young, and they have been here every day since. Each year with new kids to feed.

One has learned to mimic me and calls hello when they arrive.

This crow family is the inspiration for my tale.